I'm Going To **READ!**™

These levels are meant only as guides;
you and your child can best choose a book that's right.

Level 1: Kindergarten–Grade 1 . . . Ages 4–6
- word bank to highlight new words
- consistent placement of text to promote readability
- easy words and phrases
- simple sentences build to make simple stories
- art and design help new readers decode text

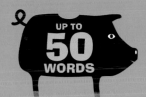

Level 2: Grade 1 . . . Ages 6–7
- word bank to highlight new words
- rhyming texts introduced
- more difficult words, but vocabulary is still limited
- longer sentences and longer stories
- designed for easy readability

Level 3: Grade 2 . . . Ages 7–8
- richer vocabulary of up to 200 different words
- varied sentence structure
- high-interest stories with longer plots
- designed to promote independent reading

Level 4: Grades 3 and up . . . Ages 8 and up
- richer vocabulary of more than 300 different words
- short chapters, multiple stories, or poems
- more complex plots for the newly independent reader
- emphasis on reading for meaning

LEVEL 3

Library of Congress Cataloging-in-Publication Data Available

2 4 6 8 10 9 7 5 3 1

Published by Sterling Publishing Co., Inc.
387 Park Avenue South, New York, NY 10016
Text copyright © 2005 by Harriet Ziefert Inc.
Illustrations copyright © 2005 by Martha Gradisher
Distributed in Canada by Sterling Publishing
c/o Canadian Manda Group, 165 Dufferin Street
Toronto, Ontario, Canada M6K 3H6
Distributed in Great Britain and Europe by Chris Lloyd at Orca Book
Services, Stanley House, Fleets Lane, Poole BH15 3AJ, England
Distributed in Australia by Capricorn Link (Australia) Pty. Ltd.
P.O. Box 704, Windsor, NSW 2756, Australia

I'm Going To Read is a trademark of Sterling Publishing Co., Inc.

Printed in China
All rights reserved
·Sterling ISBN 1-4027-2711-9

I'm Going To READ!

A Valentine for Ms. Vanilla

Pictures by Martha Gradisher

Sterling Publishing Co., Inc.
New York

It's Valentine's Day.

Ms. Vanilla puts
a valentine box
on her desk.

"Now, class," she says,
"we will make valentines."

Everybody gets busy.

Very busy.

They all make cards.

They all write poems.

One, two, three, four, five—
the box is stuffed with valentines.

"Now, class," says Ms. Vanilla.
"It's cleanup time."

"Let's clean up. Then we can have our party."

It's party time in
Ms. Vanilla's class.

Angelina hands out napkins.
Charlene hands out cupcakes.

Donald hands out
candy hearts.

And Ms. Vanilla
pours the punch.

"Now, class," says Ms. Vanilla,
"it's time to open valentines.
Lee Wong, you can pick first."

Lee Wong opens a card.

He reads:

"I will cover you with slime
If you won't be my valentine!"

Mary Ann opens a card.
She reads:

"I'll be your valentine, I think,
If you stop telling me I stink."

Donald reads his.

"Valentine, you mean more to me
Than watching cartoons on my TV."

Charlene reads hers.

"Valentine, I'll stick to you
Like chewing gum upon my shoe."

Everyone listens to Angelina.

"My valentine is never icky,
Like oatmeal when it's cold and sticky."

Next comes Paul.

"Valentine, you're not so good to eat.
But still I think you're pretty neat."

Now it's Ben's turn.

"I'll climb on Ms. Vanilla's desk,
If my valentine says she loves me best."

Melba is last.

"Roses are red, violets are blue,
Kiss Ms. Vanilla and I'll kiss you."

Then Rosa says, "Ms. Vanilla,
we made a valentine for you."

"For Ms. Vanilla we all cheer,
The greatest teacher of the year.
Here's a heart we all have signed—

Will you be
our valentine?"

Angelina Benita

MaryAnn

Max Charlene Ben

Paul Lee

Rosa Harry

Donald

Melba